The Candy Cane Killer

By Constance Barker

Similarities to real people, places or events are purely coincidental.

Sign up for Constance Barker's New Releases Newsletter

I will never spam or sell your email address

Chapter One

It was a peaceful and sunny winter's day in Paint Creek, Kentucky. But with the annual Christmas Festival starting tonight, I could taste the excitement in the air. We had gotten a beautiful and rare one-inch blanket of white snow in the morning, and it was looking and feeling like Christmas.

My favorite day of the year is just one week away! I thought as I savored the last sip of my cup of hot cocoa. My mind a million miles away as I sat in the front booth of my diner.

That was when the wicked ambush attack happened.

My brain was absorbed with relaxing thoughts and fun ideas for our concession stand at the festival, when I was suddenly startled by a clamorous thud on the plate glass window, just inches from my head. I nearly jumped out of my skin.

I looked through the remains of a shattered snowball that had just landed on the glass to see a tall, goofy-looking fellow in a Sheriff's hat and jacket with his thumbs in his ears and his tongue out, waggling his fingers at me. It was my fiancé, Sheriff Brody Hayes.

And this was war.

He waved for me to come out, and then he hollered with his hands around his mouth, “Come out here, Mercy Howard! You’re not afraid, are you?”

I wasn’t. It was such a pleasant day, I went out the door in just my sweater, hatching my plot for revenge behind my smile.

“Better watch it there, fella,” I said to him. “I happen to know the Sheriff of this county, and a prank like that could get you arrested.”

“Oh yeah?” He teased, like the sixth-grader that he seemed to be emulating today. “Well, I ain’t afraid of no Sheriff. He’s probably a sissy-boy anyway. I’ll bet a girl could beat him up.”

“Well, he’s definitely no sissy-boy,” I said, casually walking close to one of the outdoor tables. I looked at the sky to divert his attention as I gathered a handful of sticky snow from the tabletop. “But he’s afraid of girls. That’s for sure.”

That was as far as his male ego was willing to take the game, and he stepped up to me and put his ice-cold hands on my cheeks.

“If I’m afraid of girls, then how come I’m engaged to the prettiest one in town?”

His flattery was not going to work today. Not

after that surprise attack. He was expecting a kiss, but I had to string this out a little longer.

"Maybe she's just taking pity on you, Sheriff," I said flirtatiously.

He moved in for a kiss, and I made my move. A handful of icy snow was soon pressed against the back of his neck, and I shoved as much of it inside his shirt collar as I could.

I tried to run, laughing with devilish delight as I attempted my getaway. But he grabbed my arm. He took a handful of snow and held it close to my face. Time to use my superpowers. But which one? Fight? Flight? Or Mind Control? *Let's go with that one...*

I turned on my female power of persuasion (which Brody calls *the eyeball of death*), to deter him from his dirty deed. That was all it took.

Deloris stuck her head out the door.

"When you two kids are done playing, I need you to come inside and taste my hot wassail punch. Tell me what you think."

Brody and I looked at each other with eager, child-like eyes.

"Truce?"

"Truce!"

We were inside in a jiffy and followed our noses, and Deloris, into the shiny kitchen.

"I love your wassail, Deloris. Are you going to finally give me your recipe this year?"

"It's just eight gallons of pressed apple cider with a little of this and a little of that added. I'll leave it to you in my will, Mercy," she said as she took a huge boiling kettle off the stovetop and set it on the stainless-steel table next to a big stainless mixing bowl. "I don't need any competition for wassail queen just yet, so you'll just have to be patient."

"It smells fabulous!" Brody said, trying to sneak a dipper into the pot of boiling gold.

She slapped his hand. "It's not ready yet."

She gathered the top edges of a large cheesecloth that she had clothes-pinned around the rim of the pot. The rest of the mesh hung submerged in the punch, about halfway to the bottom or so, filled with fruity goodies. Then she pulled out a punching-bag-sized load of spices and fruits that had been simmering in the punch and set it in the mixing bowl, still in the cheesecloth. When the top of the cloth fell open, I could see several large oranges studded with whole cloves, large slices of fresh pineapple, a couple of lemons cut in half, and the remains of several cinnamon sticks.

She cut the oranges open, then took another bowl and pressed down on all the fruits to squeeze out more of the juice. Then she pulled the cheese cloth with the ingredients out, letting all the juice drip out, and tossed it away. There was probably a cup or two of juice in the bowl, which she poured into the large kettle of wassail and stirred it up.

"Now it's ready."

She ladled two cupfuls into large mugs for Brody and me.

"Just one cup each, guys. This is going to the Old School Diner concession stand at Christmas Festival tonight for charity. I'll be making another batch every day of the festival, though."

"Okay!" I said with a smile. "Thank you!" And we ran into the dining room like a couple of kids anxious for Santa to come.

"Wow!" Brody said as he took a sip of the hot concoction. "I've heard you rave about it, but I had no idea this stuff was so good! It tastes like..."

"Christmas!" I inhaled the warm steam wafting off my cup with my eyes closed and dreamed of gingerbread men and sugar plum fairies, just like when I was a girl.

"You're right. That's exactly what it tastes like, Mercy." He took another sip and smiled at me. "So, let's go to the town festival tonight. Opening night – they'll be lighting the tree. And there'll be hay rides and food and music…"

"…and handcrafted gifts and ornaments – I get one every year," I added. "And, of course, Santa will be there tonight too. I'm in!"

Paint Creek is a sleepy, small town in Kentucky, not far from the Indiana border, where I grew up. After several years as an ER nurse in the big city, I came home to run the little diner that my grandfather had opened 50 years ago. I'm really glad I did.

"You can't have wassail without some Christmas cookies," Deloris said, coming in from the kitchen. "Babsy baked these this morning before she left to run the concession stand."

Deloris was my lovable but cranky counter manager who had pretty much run the place for the past 30 years. Babs waited on the tables and booths, and she lived in the little apartment upstairs.

"I get the star with the chocolate kiss in the middle!" I said, claiming my cookie and taking a big bite immediately.

"And I'll take all the rest of them!" Brody teased – at least, I thought he was teasing.

Deloris folded up an old yellowed piece of paper, which said *Aunt Lydia's Hot Wassail Punch* on the top. She stuck it right about in the center of her tall blonde beehive hairdo, which she used as a purse. You never knew what she might pull out of there. I've seen everything from photographs, to lipstick, to playing cards, to half a sandwich, to a semi-automatic pistol come out of that nest.

"Are you coming out to the festival tonight, Deloris?" Brody asked her. "Or would you like us to bring the punch there for you?"

"Oh, I'll be going there, alright. I got roped into being an elf in Santa's Wonderland with all those pesky kids lining up all night."

"Oh, that's wonderful!" I said. "Red's an elf too, isn't he? And Jake too. So that should be fun!"

"Fun, shmun," she griped. "Just a lot of spoiled little rug rats hyped up on sugar candy, running around on the loose and hollering. Parents these days don't watch their kids, just let them go wild."

That wasn't true here in Paint Creek, but Deloris had her cantankerous image to keep up. She loved the kids and I knew she was excited.

"What about Santa?" I asked. "Did Junior finally find a Santa suit? He's been growing his beard out since school started, so he should look pretty authentic if he can find a nice suit."

"No idea, Mercy. I found some little green lederhosen and a candy-striped blouse for myself, and Red says he has a pointy cap for me. But all I got to do is pass out candy canes for the tiny terrorists."

My chin slipped off my hand, as I had fallen asleep right there at the counter. It caught Brody's attention as I jerked back into consciousness,

"Are you alright, Mercy?" He was more concerned than necessary. "I think you've been working too hard lately, burning the candle at both ends to get the booth ready for the festival."

"Oh, no, Brody." I appreciated his concern, but I was fine. "Just tired. I always get anxious and have trouble sleeping this close to Christmas. It brings back so many childhood memories – and memories of my loved ones who are gone now. That's all."

He pulled me close. "Well, we'll get you to bed early tonight."

Deloris rolled her eyes.

"It sounds like your whole crew is going to be running Santa's Wonderland, Mercy." Brody said. "Who's going to be running the diner?"

"That would be me," Smoke said walking out of the kitchen with a cup of wassail. Smoke was granddad's original chef, almost since the day he opened.

His punch smelled of rum, which is the way my dad always liked it too. “The whole town will be at the festival all week, so I can cook and take orders too. Won’t be a problem.”

I felt bad for Smoke having to stay behind all by himself. “Well, if it’s dead, just lock up and come to the festival, Smoke.”

“I’ll be fine – but I will be coming out for the big Parade of Lights at sundown on Christmas Eve.”

“Of course. We’ll close at 4:00 on Christmas Eve.”

Chapter Two

It was almost the winter solstice – the shortest day of the year – so it was already dark when we got to the festival grounds. It was all the way across town from the Old School Diner – about seven blocks – and it looked like the whole town was there, at the town square at the end of the commercial district.

Actually, the town square wasn't square at all. It was a beautiful park set in a full circle, maybe about 150 yards in diameter. You might say it was a huge grassy island in the middle of a big *cul de sac* at the end of Main Street.

I know it was longer than a football field, because they set up a temporary field with bleachers there when they tore down the old high school stadium and rebuilt it when I was still in grade school. The road had cars parked all the way around the circle already.

The north side of the circle had a beautifully decorated and lighted Christmas Market that looked like an old-fashioned village. It reminded me of the one my grandfather built around his beloved train set in his basement. There were houses, stores, and a church, all white with red roofs. The structures were built of heavy plywood with hinges holding the walls together, so they could collapse and be stored easily. There were also white tents set up for more merchants at each end of the little town.

The wide street down the center of the village had an occasional horse, usually followed by an elf with a shovel and wheel barrow. And there was a family of carolers dressed in attire right out of a Charles Dickens novel. They were singing *We Wish You a Merry Christmas* when they passed by the Old School booth, where I had stopped by to visit Babs. Brody said he had to "check something" and he would join me shortly.

"How's business, Babs? Do you have everything you need?"

"Oh, goodness, yes, Mercy!" She said with her usual bright smile as she collected $3 for three cups of wassail.

"The punch is popular, of course. We will sell a hundred cups or so every night for the veterans' club, so that should make them happy. And your idea for empanadas was genius! They're all made at the diner ahead of time, stashed away in our little freezer here, and deep fried to order. No work, and lots of choices! I think we will need to do more sloppy joe and chili ones for tomorrow, though. The chicken pot pie and pizza ones are doing real well too, but the veggie and cheese ones are slow movers."

I felt a kiss on my cheek.

"Who's there?" I teased Brody when he came up behind me. I turned and saw that he was holding a ball of mistletoe over my head. "You know, if you play your cards right, you won't need the mistletoe."

"Good to know!" He said and handed me a very small white gift bag with a bow on top.

"For me?" I asked with a smile.

Brody looked around. "I don't see anyone else here, so I must be talking to you," he said in a bad DeNiro impression.

I tried to hide my eyeroll and opened the bag.

"Ah! It's an ornament for my Christmas tree!" I said, holding up a five-inch porcelain candy cane with a beautiful gold bow and the year dangling from the bottom.

"Thank you, Brody. That was very thoughtful. I love it!" And I did. "You know this is my first ornament as an engaged woman, so it's very special coming from you."

"I was thinking you might like something colorful that reminds you of your childhood Christmases. And you know, there's a good chance that this will be your *only* ornament as an engaged woman."

I had to think about that for a moment. "So, I guess by next Christmas I'll either be a jilted ex-fiancé, or..."

"...or a married woman. Merry Christmas, sweetheart."

Suddenly, red and green searchlights at the center of the park began flooding the night sky, swirling and turning, lighting up the clouds and trees and everything all around the park. They finally stopped, fixing their aim on the big unlit tree far away in the middle of the circle, and then they slowly moved upward to form a sort of teepee around the tree. Then they all moved straight up, and then slightly outward, away from the tree, so the area was lighted for the people, but the tree was still in darkness.

The town crier started ringing his bell, telling us that the lighting ceremony was about to begin.

There was a beautiful fountain in the center of the park in the summertime, but tonight that is where they would be lighting the 30-foot Christmas tree that was all decorated and ready to go. And best of all, Santa would be making his debut! He would flip the switch, and then Santa's Wonderland would be open. The kids were already lining up.

"We better get moving, Brody. That's farther than it looks. Don't want to miss the lighting! See you, Babs! Let me know if you need anything!"

Mayor Bud Finster was on the raised platform, right between the big Christmas tree and the entryway to Santa's Wonderland.

The curtains to Santa's place were pulled shut behind the big candy cane arches that formed the gate, and the kids – ok, all of us – were eager to see Santa come out and up the steps onto the Stage.

Bud was tapping the microphone, which seemed to be working fine, and the spotlights came up to full brightness. There was a drum set, guitars, and amplifiers behind him for the band that would be playing soon.

On the other side of the stage by the tree was the high school marching band, in uniform with instruments poised.

A lovely girl in her early teens made her way onto the stage in a white dress trimmed in red satin, and Bud greeted her warmly. Her sash said

Christmas Angel.

A siren from the firetruck on exhibit not far away sounded one time, indicating that it was 7:00 p.m. and time to begin. The footlights on the front of the stage came on, and Bud approached the mic stand.

"Howdy, there, Creekers and visitors from around the area! Welcome to the kickoff of our annual Paint Creek Christmas Festival!"

The band played the first few rousing bars of *We Wish You a Merry Christmas*. Then they stopped, and the crowd applauded. Bud described some of the events and festivities.

Then the crowd started shouting for Santa Claus.

"Where's Santa?"

"Yeah! We want Santa Claus!"

"Santa! Santa! Santa!"

Bud made downward motions with his hands to calm the crowd, and then admonitions of, "Shh! Shh! Shh!" could be heard from the crowd as it quieted down.

"You'll meet Santa soon enough. But first I want you to meet the young lady who is going to introduce Santa for you. Ladies and gentlemen, please welcome this year's winner of Paint Creek's Christmas Angel Pageant, and our mascot for the festival. From Paint Creek Junior High School, please welcome Miss Katie Ann Holloway!"

The band played again briefly as the crowd cheered and applauded.

"Oh!" I whispered to Brody. "I'll bet that's Teddy Holloway's little girl! Isn't she adorable?"

Brody nodded.

"Congratulations, Katie Ann," Bud said. "And, well, every angel has to have her wings. So now, on behalf of the village of Paint Creek, I would like to present you with your Christmas Angel wings!"

More music. More clapping. Bud put the toy store wings on the little girl.

Brody gave me an odd look. "Those look more like butterfly wings, than angel wings, don't they?"

"Actually, they're fairy princess wings."

He gave me another odd look, but I didn't flinch.

"It takes a trained eye to tell them apart."

Finally, the moment came, and he gave Katie

the microphone. All she said was:

"Heeeeeere's Santa Claus!"

The spotlights flooded the gate to Santa's Wonderland as the curtains opened and the band played *Here Comes Santa Claus.*

The crowd clapped and cheered, and Santa's elves took the stage first. It was our Deloris first, looking very elf-ish, followed by two of our favorite regulars at the diner, Red and Jake.

Red is in his 70s now and has a crush on Deloris. Jake is still under 50, portly, not very tall, and the owner of Carter & Son Construction Company with his son, Junior, who shares his body type.

Then we heard the first ho-ho-hos and saw an arm waving as Junior came up the steps to the stage. The crowd became uncharacteristically quiet. White powder was wafting off his black beard as he walked to the microphone in...red pajamas!

"Merrrrry Christmas!" Junior said convincingly into the microphone, but the crowd wasn't having it.

"Where's your Santa Suit?" A child called out from in front of the stage.

"My suit? Well, um...it was at the cleaners, and Prancer is bringing it in, special delivery, first thing in the morning! Ho ho ho! I thought it might be kind of fun for you all to see how Santa dresses when he's at home!"

It was a disaster, but it didn't deter the kids from lining up to sit on his lap. I mean, he was a wonderful Santa, he really was, but the disappointment of the kids was obvious.

The tree did look beautiful, though. When Santa flipped the switch that brought back most of the merriment.

Santa and his elves had just waved their goodbyes on their way to Wonderland and the band had stopped playing when we heard a shrill, shrieking scream from a woman at the life-sized nativity scene near the east side of the park.

"What is she screaming?" I asked Brody?

He looked quite alarmed as he grabbed my arm and started running. "I think she's screaming, *Bloody murder!*"

Chapter Three

The Sheriff's Department was providing security for the event, so there were already several cruisers at the venue, as well as ambulance and fire. The nativity was quickly surrounded with flashing lights, and a deputy was cordoning off a perimeter around it with yellow tape, attaching it to trees and road-block sawhorses. The people were kept back at least 20 feet, but I went in with Brody.

"She's an ER nurse," Brody said to a deputy I hadn't seen before.

"Go on ahead in, Sheriff, but I doubt if a nurse is going to be able to do anything for this guy. He looks pretty dead." The officer just kept chewing his gum and seemed very dispassionate, which I suppose is good in law enforcement.

"Oh, my gosh!" I said as we approached the body.

A well-dressed man in his 50s was lying on his back, eyes still open. He was laid out in front of the manger with what must have been a two-foot long candy cane plunged through his chest.

An EMT was kneeling over him, waiting for the crime team.

"He's dead," he told Brody and me.

I pointed to the murder weapon. "Is that a real candy cane?"

"I don't know. Want to take a lick?" He said, snorting a couple of times. "Sorry, ma'am. CSI humor. Actually, no, but it looks pretty real. It's a real walking cane, though. I've seen a few of them around tonight." He pointed to the bottom 12 inches of the cane a few feet away. "That part is a sheath for a foot-long blade that allows you to use the cane kind of like a sword, or maybe a letter opener, I guess. Must be custom-made though, 'cause the ones they sell in the Christmas Market here are one solid piece. I was able to see that the blade goes all the way through him when I was checking to see if he was still alive."

"Wait!" I said, looking at the man's familiar face. "Isn't that the news anchor from Channel 7?"

"I think so," the young man said. "yeah pretty sure this is Ed Greely."

Suddenly I felt dizzy and a little nauseous. I

wasn't ready for another murder – not now; not right before Christmas. The world was spinning, and it was difficult to stand up. I could feel my knees going weak, so I took a step back and took a hold of Brody's hand. I think I actually fell asleep for a brief moment, but everything looked a little brighter and better when I opened my eyes.

"Brody..."

"Yes, dear?"

"I'm...it's, um, Christmas, and, you know..."

"I know. You don't want to be tracking down a killer and thinking about this bloody scene. I don't want you to either."

"Are you sure? I mean, we work so well together on these things." I was feeling a lot better already.

"We do. I might ask for your opinion on some things from time to time. You need your rest, and no stress for a while. You've been working too hard and missing meals for two weeks now. Besides, you've got a more important mission right now."

"I do? What's that?"

"Well, besides running the busiest concession stand at the festival and running a diner too, I saw your brain working overtime when Junior showed up in red pajamas. You have to find Santa a real

Santa suit – a proper one, worthy of a great Santa like Junior."

He was right. That's exactly what I wanted to do. I don't know how, but he was really tuned into my every thought and need right now.

"Why don't you head over to Santa's workshop now and see how the gang is doing, Merse? I'll wait for the medical examiner and crime team. We'll be here late, because we'll want to get a photograph of everyone in the area before they leave, but we'll do our best not to interfere with the fun of the festival."

I smiled at him. No wonder I loved this man.

"Meet me there later?"

"Will do."

I practically ran back to Santa's Wonderland. Something felt different tonight. Good different. Maybe it was the Christmas spirit. I felt light as a feather as I ran, and I arrived there in no time at all, almost like Scotty beamed me up.

It was very busy at Santa's place. The kids didn't seem to mind the red pajamas anymore, though the parents were still whispering about it.

A little boy, about 5, was sitting on Junior's lap, punching him in the tummy. "Is that your real fat belly, Santa? Last year Santa had a pillow under his shirt."

"Ho ho ho, little one! That's my bowl full of jelly!"

Junior grabbed his belly with both hands and shook it. It jiggled wildly, much to the child's delight. As for me, I was wondering how I could "unsee" it.

Deloris was making her way down the line of children, handing out candy canes. She bent over, putting her hands on her knees to talk to one really cute little gal.

"What's your name, sweetheart?"

I couldn't hear the meek response, but I listened to Deloris for a while.

"Oh, my! Cassandra is a lovely name. You must be about 7, I think."

The girl nodded.

"Well, I've got a special treat for a big girl like you. Do you like chocolate?"

The girl jumped a little and clapped her tiny hands one time.

Deloris gave her a few pieces of foil-wrapped chocolate and had a huge smile when she turned to see me standing with my arms folded behind her.

She stopped smiling.

“So, how are the awful little monsters treating you tonight, Deloris?”

She walked away from the line to talk to me. “What are you looking so smug about, Mercy Howard? They’re awful, as usual, but I’ve been on my best behavior.”

“I see that. Who’s the little darling you gave the chocolate kisses too?”

“That’s Cassandra Breen. I suppose she has some potential as a decent human being. So, what’s all the fuss down by the nativity scene?”

I winced. “It’s not good. I’ll tell you all about it later. Where’s Jake?”

“Oh, he’s in the big barn out back, trying to get the old wagon ready for hay rides. Hopefully he’ll have it working by tomorrow. It’s got a broken axel. Red’s taking a nap with the invisible reindeer, so it’s just me and Junior holding down the fort.”

“Good, then. I’ll let you get back to your drudgery with the children of the corn.”

I noticed a very lean young pre-teen girl lurking several paces from Santa’s big chair, just behind Junior’s peripheral vision. She had been watching him very closely, and now she was glancing at me repeatedly. She looked to be 11 or

12, with spindly, lanky arms and legs – but still healthy-looking. And, well, she had rather pointy ears sticking out from under her hay-colored straight hair.

Maybe "lurking" is the wrong word, as she really didn't seem sinister. I felt compelled to go over and talk to her, so I made my way around the back of Santa's throne.

"Hi!" I said cheerfully, not wanting to frighten her. "I'm Mercy Howard. Are you one of Santa's elves?"

She giggled. "A pixie, actually."

Her big green baby-doll eyes were like bottomless pools of joy, and I thought I was going to fall into them.

"He's really a wonderful Santa Claus, you know," she said with a timid smile. "And I've seen the best – the real St. Nick himself."

"Right, well, he is great with the kids, and he has such a kind and generous heart," I said. "I just have to help him find a good Santa suit tomorrow, so he can look like the great Santa he is. Maybe the department store will have one."

"No. A department store suit will not do." She looked at me now like she was sizing me up for some reason. She looked at Junior as he warmly brought another child onto his lap and then reached into her pocket.

"Here," she said, handing me a green business card made of translucent plastic.

I looked at the unique card, which had red ribbon printed around the border with a candy cane at the very top. It just said *Cupcake* at the top, and in the center of the card it said *Ferdinand's Mystical Emporium*.

"So, you are..."

"Cupcake, yes. That's me." Her eyes diverted downward. "My parents wanted a girl."

"Oh! So, you are..."

He looked a little upset now.

"I mean, of course I know you're a *boy*. It's a good masculine name, really."

He smiled. "Do you really think so?"

"Well, it fits you, and you're, you know, quite...masculine."

"But I'm not a boy. I'm a man. I'm 35. Promise me you will take this Santa Claus there in the morning, Mercy," he said, pointing at the card.

I just looked at his eyes again. I felt like I really wanted to go there as soon as possible.

"Promise me." He took my hand in his oddly warm, silky hands.

"Yes! Yes, of course, Cupcake. But...how do I get there?"

"Just turn right when you see the wooden windmill right after you cross the old bridge over Paint Creek. Ask for Ferdy. Ferdy will give you the right suit."

I knew the windmill, and there was no road there.

"But..."

"Just follow the card, Mercy. The card will get you there."

I felt like I could trust him, as I looked at the card and rubbed my thumb across his name.

"Okay, Cupcaaa...."

He was gone! I looked up, left, right behind me. There was no sign of Cupcake. If I hadn't still had the odd calling card in my hand, I would have thought I was going crazy.

"Ho ho ho!" Junior said to the kids. "Santa's got to go and feed Rudolph and the other reindeer now! I'll be back in 15 minutes! Be good for Santa, now! Ho ho ho!"

I followed him out behind the Wonderland set. Red was sound asleep on a bench in the back.

"Junior!"

"Hi, Mercy. I was getting kind of hungry, so I was just going to run the Old School booth to get a snack."

My phone rang. It was my neighbor and best friend, Ruby Owana.

"Hi, Mercy! I'm at the Old School concession stand looking for you."

"Great! I said. "Grab a couple Philly cheese steak empanadas for Junior and come to the big barn behind Santa's Wonderland. Junior just has a few minutes."

"And two beef stew ones and a ham and cheese!" Junior said loud enough for her to hear.

"I'll be right there!"

"Thanks, Mercy. It would have been awkward for me to walk over there in my Santa outfit."

"That's what I want to talk to you about, Junior. Let's go see how your dad is doing with the hay wagon."

I told him to be at the diner early for breakfast, and then we would go and find him the prefect Santa suit.

"But we'll eat breakfast first, right, Mercy?"

"Yes, Junior. And when we get back we'll have your second breakfast."

"K. But I've checked all the thrift shops, and I couldn't find anything. I finally found these red pajamas at the Supersavers Mart in Ballers Ferry."

"Well, I got a tip that we might find one at some shop by the old windmill."

"The old windmill? There's nothing out there but swamp and quack grass."

I pulled on the big barn door of the old shed, but it wouldn't budge.

Junior put his big hand on the end of the door, flicked his wrist, and it opened right up. "It slides, Mercy."

"Thanks." I didn't bother telling him that I was trying to slide it.

"Dang! Dang! Dang!"

Jake was obviously frustrated and irritated when we found him inside. I heard a hammer or wrench or something banging onto some kind of metal underneath the big wagon he was trying to get ready for the hay ride.

“What’s the problem, Pops?” Junior asked his dad.

“The axel is not only broken in two, but its totally rusted right to the wheel hubs. I just don’t know how we’re going to get this thing moving, son.”

“No problem,” Junior told him. “It’s Christmas. We don’t need a hay ride; we need a sleigh ride. I’ll bring the torch tomorrow. We can cut those wheels off and put some runners on it.”

Jake and I looked at each other. I let his dad do the talking.

“Junior, this is Kentucky. That inch of snow we got this morning is almost gone. And, that was probably close to half the snowfall we’ll get all winter long.”

Junior didn’t flinch. “Sometimes we get more. Besides, I’m Santa, and Santa needs a sleigh. We’ve already got some horse that we can dress up like reindeer, and I’ll drive the sleigh.”

“We can’t do all that by tomorrow...”

“We’ll get it done as soon as we can. For sure, it’ll be done in time for the Parade of Lights on Christmas Eve.”

“Hello-oo!” Ruby sang as she came inside with Junior’s snack. “Look who I brought with me!

Lucille was looking for you, so I brought her here for you, Mercy."

Lucille Gildemeister was the one who organized the whole festival every year. She was a very professional and sophisticated lady.

"Oh, thank God I found you, Mercy," she said, quite animated and, it appeared, on a mission.

"Hi, Lu..."

"Well, my daughter-in-law, Marcy, just informed me that she is going skiing in Aspen and won't be able to manage the Parade."

"The Parade of Li...?"

"Imagine that! So, it got me thinking, who can I get on short notice who can pull this off?"

"Who?" *Oh, no...*

"So, I thought Marcy – Mercy! That's it! Mercy Howard!"

"But..."

"I know you'll do a wonderful job, Mercy."

Oh, there is absolutely no way...

"It's a great opportunity for you, and the whole town is counting on a fabulous parade. I can't really depend on anyone else. We wouldn't want to ruin Christmas for everyone, now, would we? So, what do you say, Mercy? Will you produce the parade for me?"

Absolutely not!

"Wha...why, of course, Lucille! I'd love to! It would be an honor."

She patted me on the shoulder. "Good girl. The participants are all set, the funding is taken care of. You just have to make sure they're ready and in compliance with all of the rules. Then, just line them all up, and make it go! This old bucket of bolts will have to be ready to carry Santa, too," she said, patting the side of the wagon. "I'll have the requirements and entrant list sent to your little café in the morning." Then she turned and left.

I looked at Ruby with panic in my eyes, and more of it in the pit of my stomach.

What just happened here?

"Thanks so much for bringing Lucille to see me, Ruby. Oh – and thanks for volunteering to be my Assistant Producer, Miss Owana."

Chapter Four

I don't even remember sleeping. I guess between the stress of becoming the producer for the town's big parade and my excitement to find that Santa suit, I was getting a little scatter-brained. And the funny thing was, I didn't feel tired or stressed out at all.

Next thing I knew, I was at the diner watching Junior and his dad chomp down pancakes by the plateful along with enough sausage and bacon to make the average person sprout a curly tail.

"Day's a wasting," I said to Junior. "Get a cup of coffee to go, and let's hit the road."

He looked at his watch. "It's just 7:15, Mercy. Most places won't even be open yet.

I gave him the eyeball of death.

"But I'm ready," he said. Crumpling his napkin and tossing it on his empty plate. "I'm all coffeed out though. Let's take my Rav. I don't think your little roadster will do too well driving through that swamp."

I thought his dad was going to spit coffee across the counter. "Now, why on earth would you two be driving through a swamp in the middle of winter in Kentucky?"

"Oh, we're not going *in* the swamp, Jake." *I don't think.* "We're just going out by the river. Come on, Junior."

I turned on the radio in the car to get some music, but the news was on.

"Oh, they're talking about the murder of Ed Greely." I turned the volume up a little.

"They're calling him the Candy Cane Killer. But there are still no suspects in the unusual murder of Channel 7 anchorman Ed Greely in Paint Creek last night. In a news conference this morning, Sheriff Hayes said that the victim's name had been engraved on the blade of the murder weapon."

"The Candy Cane Killer," Junior said. "That's kind of catchy. If I was going to get murdered, that's who I'd want to kill me."

Junior was one of a kind.

We were almost to the old bridge over Paint Creek, just outside of town, when I decided I'd better take a look at Cupcake's business card. Maybe there was an address.

The clear red plastic felt warm in my hand. *I could have sworn this card was green with a red ribbon.* Now, however, it was red with a green ribbon. It said, *Ferdinand's Mystical Emporium, Next Right Turn.*

"That's odd," I mumbled to myself.

"What's that, Mercy?" Junior asked. "There's the old windmill. We'll be crossing the bridge in a second."

As we bumped across the old wooden bridge, the card seemed to get brighter. *Turn Right 50 Feet,* the card said.

I'm losing my mind.

Then the card started flashing and displayed only a large white arrow.

"Here," I told Junior.

I'm not sure if he turned the wheel or if it turned by itself, but soon we were bouncing off the road, blinded by bushes and the low-hanging branches of a weeping willow tree. I was sure we would soon be dead or stuck in the muck forever. Then, suddenly, after a couple more bumps and thuds, we were on a bright, wide gravel road that went perfectly straight ahead into the rising sun.

"Huh." Junior scratched his head. "I spent a lot of years catching frogs right here when I was a kid, but I never knew this road was here."

Exactly one mile later, we pulled up in front of the little shop. It was sitting all by itself in the middle of nowhere, and ours was the only car there.

Junior pointed to the door. "The sign says *Open.*"

The wooden structure looked like something out of the old west. It had a wide, open front porch, the whole width of the storefront, with rails around the front and sides.

"I guess this is where people tie their horses," he said with a smile filled with child-like wonder.

The long metal sign above the door was very decorative and nicely painted. It just said *Emporium* in large red letters, and beneath the name it said, *We sell everything – Just ask!*

The bell above the door jingled as we entered. There was a man with spectacles behind the counter, leaning on one elbow and working on some papers on a clipboard. He was dressed in a white shirt with black suspenders attached to his black slacks.

"Looks like we're the only customers, Junior."

"I don't see anything that looks like a Santa suit, though, Mercy. Looks like a lot of old used books and rusty tools and junk."

The man looked up at us but didn't smile. He looked at us both, up and down, several times.

"Let me guess," he said, rubbing his chin, still looking at me and Junior, and then me again.

"Excuse me?" I asked.

He waved his hand, indicating that I shouldn't bother him while he's thinking, I guess.

"Are you Ferdy? I'm looking for Ferdy."

He nodded. "I've got it!" He announced with a triumphant smile. "You are here for a lamp! The wishing lamp of the genie of Araby!"

I looked confused, and shook my head.

"No...no," he said, scratching his head. "Let me think...let me think...let me think. Aha! You want a chicken that lays golden eggs! That's it!"

"No, sir. I..."

"A mirror that will tell you you're the fairest in the land?"

"No," I said, handing him Cupcake's card, which was green again. "I'm looking for..."

"Ahhhhh!" He said with an enormous smile, turning his gaze to Junior now. "You're the one! You're here for Santa's suit. I'll get it for you."

He quickly disappeared into the back room, and Junior and I looked at each other.

"I hope it's a good suit, Junior."

"As long as it's red with white cuffs and stuff."

The man came back out with a large red box, perhaps two-and-a-half feet square, and 18 inches deep. There was a red and green ribbon around the box, culminating in a bow at the center with several shiny bells attached.

He blew some dust off the top and slid the huge carton across the counter. It looked like a Christmas gift, and I was eager to see what was inside.

"Can we open it?" I asked, already reaching for the ribbon. I looked at Junior. "In a box this big, it's not going to be one of those flimsy suits. I'll bet it's a good one."

The man grabbed my wrist to keep me from

sliding the ribbon off. “Santa must open the box,” he said.

Junior slid the ribbon off quickly and lifted the cover. His eyes went wide, and my jaw dropped. It was almost as if angels started singing and beams of light shot out from the box around the lush red velvety suit. Junior looked at me, and I nodded for him to take it out.

He picked it up by the shoulders, and it unfolded for all of us to see.

“Oh, my Gosh!”

I was amazed to see the thick, luxurious, velvety fabric, the brightest red I’d ever seen.

“Is that white trim real rabbit fur?” I asked Ferdy.

“Ermine, Ma’am, yes.”

“And look at those shiny brass buttons!”

“24-karat gold electroplate.”

The pants were the same fabric, and there was a 4-inch wide black leather belt and pointy Santa cap beneath them. On the bottom of the box was a pair of black leather boots with gold buckles.

“What size are the boots?” Junior asked.

"They're your size," the man told him with a confident grin.

"This is the most magnificent Santa suit I've ever seen!" I said, rubbing the plush fabric on my face.

"It's not a Santa suit, Miss – this is Santa's actual suit. The real one."

I rolled my eyes just slightly. "Well doesn't Santa need it?" I asked, trying to hide my sarcasm.

"He's Santa," Ferdy said pointing to Junior.

Junior wasn't one to show excitement, but he was beaming now. "Can I try it on?"

"It's required, actually," he said, gesturing toward the changing room. "We have to make sure it works."

"Works?" I asked, a bit confused. "You mean fits."

"Of course, it will fit, Miss. The question is, is this man the one? Will the suit accept him as Santa."

"Be right back," Junior said disappearing into the dressing room with the suit.

Everything was most unusual, yet it all seemed perfectly normal somehow.

"Ho ho ho ho ho ho ho!"

Junior's boisterous voice boomed from the dressing room.

"It sounds like Junior is filled with the Christmas spirit," I said to Ferdy, who was working on his clipboard again.

"Well, I should think so. After all, he is Santa Claus now," he said without looking up or cracking a smile.

A few seconds later, Junior came out, looking like St. Nick himself. His belly was bigger and rounder, and his black beard and hair were white as snow, with no sign of powdery fallout.

"Ho ho ho!" he said walking right up to me. "Why, it's Mercy Howard! Still as pretty as the day I brought you those Rossignol Avalanche Hyper-glide snow skis – oh! And Malibu Barbie and GI Joe with the Kung-Fu grip. I hope you liked them."

"Junior, I got those when I was 8! You were born when I was 8. How...?"

Ferdy looked at me oddly. "GI Joe?"

"Well, Ken was never my type, and I was kind of a tomboy. I mean...no, of course not. He's making that up!"

"Right, mmhm."

Junior winked at me and whispered, "I guess we'd better not tell him about those Eagle Crest High School romance books, hey, Mercy? Ho ho."

"Junior! Those weren't romance books. They were Christian books for young ladies...girls...lady girls."

It was time to change the subject.

"Junior, I didn't see a fake beard in the box. How did you get your beard and hair so long and white?"

Ferdy rolled his eyes.

Junior sat down in an antique rocking chair next to us and pulled me onto his lap. Oddly, it didn't seem weird at all. "Don't you believe in Santa anymore, Mercy?"

"Um, no."

"Tsk, tsk, tsk. It's a shame. All the joy of Christmas goes away when a little girl stops believing. How can we fix this? Aha! You don't think Santa's beard is real? Do you see any strings around my ears to hold up a fake beard Mercy? Do you?"

"Well, no. That's why..."

"So, what are you waiting for? Give it a yank. Well, go ahead. Pull it!"

So now I'm little Natalie Wood in Miracle on 34th Street?

I pulled it – hard.

"Ouch!"

"Seems the suit is working," Ferdy said.

Junior was still in full character as we got up from the chair. He leaned back on his heels and slapped his belly with both hands, ho-ho-hoing as he did. Then he leaned forward.

"So, tell, me, Mercy, what would you like from Santa this year?"

"I think we should just go, Junior. You're probably getting hungry by now, and I didn't eat any breakfast. I could use a Kit Kat bar right about now to tide me over." I actually wasn't hungry at all, but I figured I should be.

He reached into his front pocket and pulled something out. "Here you go, young lady. One Kit Kat bar."

He gave me the candy bar, but nothing seemed to faze me anymore.

"Thanks."

Then he went back into the dressing room to change, laughing all the way.

I looked at Ferdy now. This fabulous suit was going to cost me a fortune. "So, how much do I owe you?"

He held up Cupcake's green calling card. "Paid in full."

"But..."

"Off with you now! I'm expecting an ornery river troll looking for a billy goat to eat."

A blink or two later, and we were back at the diner.

"Deloris, did you put LSD in my coffee this morning?"

"Whatsa matter, Merse? Your eyeballs playing tricks on you?"

"Something like that."

She had the little TV turned on to follow the news of the Candy Cane Killer, and she turned it up as the noon newscast began.

"McLean County Sheriff Brody Hayes has released four people after questioning, as the dragnet for Ed Greely's killer comes up empty," Maria Brown-Calderone said to the camera. *"More interviews of potential suspects are expected*

throughout the day."

"Sounds like Brody is going to be busy all day," I said glumly. I was getting bored and needed a playmate. "I wish the snow had stayed around longer. I was hoping for a white Christmas. Maybe Ruby can come out and play."

"This just in," Calderone said, pressing her fingers to her earpiece and listening to the producer. *"Breaking now! Another victim of the Candy Cane killer has just been discovered, this time on the state college campus in Calhoun. Mass Communications Professor Andrea Hern has been found, stabbed and placed under the campus Christmas tree in front of the student center. Like Greely, she had a candy cane sword through her heart. This is the second in what looks like a series of killings, presumably by the so-called Candy Cane Killer."*

"Oh, no! This can't be happening."

"Just what we need," Deloris said, shaking her head. "We'll have the whole area in a panic, right before Christmas while people finish up their last-minute shopping. Everyone's going to be afraid to go outside."

"This is just terrible," I said getting up from the counter. "I'm going to help Babs and Smoke make the rest of the empanadas for the festival tonight; then I'm going to call Brody and see how he's doing. Maybe I'll wait an hour, since he's got another murder now. Did you make your punch, Deloris?"

"All done. There's a small pan on the back burner with a a cup or two for you."

"You're the best," Deloris," I said, slipping through the swinging doors to the kitchen, but I could still hear Deloris's response.

"Yeah, I know that, Merse. I know that."

Chapter Five

I had been at the diner most of the day going over the notes from Lucille Gildemeister on the Parade. I contacted everyone who had signed up to enter a float, car, group, or marching band in the parade.

Ronnie Town from Town's End Hardware was the only one who said he was dropping out. He just hadn't had the time to work on his float. But I talked him into renting a convertible with a sign for his business on the doors, and I lined up a couple of the Christmas Angel runners-up to sit in the back and wave. The parade was at night, so he was required to decorate the car with a few strings of Christmas lights. He had paint at his store for the door signs that would glow in the dark.

The volunteer fire department was glad I reminded them about the parade. They were going to take the big ladder truck out and throw candy to the kids, which they hadn't bought yet.

77 exhibits in all were set for the parade, and I had to inspect every one of them before Christmas Eve. The Parade of Lights would start at the Town Square, go through Paint Creek all the way to the East End Shopping Center, and then come back using a different route, ending with a full circle around the festival grounds.

"I better check in with Babs at the festival," I said to Deloris.

"She's doing fine, Mercy. She's got 300 empanadas, a tub of coleslaw, and a dozen bags of French fries, and it's only five o'clock. Things don't really get into gear there until Santa arrives at 7:00."

"You're right, of course, Deloris, but..."

She gave me her knowing look. "But you just want to go to the festival and immerse yourself in Christmas."

"Maaaaybe. I sure hope we get a nice snow fall for Christmas. I love white Christmases. I'm going to call Ruby and see if she wants to go."

It was nice having a best friend who was off for all the holidays and summers. Ruby was the history teacher at the high school, and they started their Christmas break a few days ago. And she loved Christmas just as much as I did.

I had to wait for her candy-cane-shaped

Danish to come out of the oven, and she wanted me to stop by to look at it. She was just taking it out when I let myself in the side door by her kitchen.

"Mmm, that smells wonderful, Ruby!" It really did.

She waved me over to the table. "Come take a look, Mercy." I could see she was excited about it.

"Oh, my goodness, Ruby! You are a master baker and an artist too."

The cookie sheet had a cane-shaped pastry, perfectly browned, with diagonal stripes showing the red cherry filling.

"There's brown sugar and cinnamon under the pastry strips between the cherries," she said. "When it cools, I'll drizzle white icing there between the rows of cherries, so it will look like a real candy cane."

"It already does," I said. "Will there be peppermint in the icing?" I raised my eyebrows a couple of times.

"Oh, what a good idea! There will be now! But I'll need to get some peppermint extract."

"Or we can crush up a couple of those candy canes that Deloris passes out to the kiddos. Let's go!"

The tree was lit, and the sky was almost dark when we arrived at the town square.

"Oh, wow, Ruby! Look at that. Children are holding hands all around the Christmas tree. That song they're singing sounds familiar."

Fah who foraze! Dah who doraze!
Welcome Christmas, come this way!
Fah who foraze! Dah who doraze!
Welcome Christmas, Christmas Day!

"Of course, it does, Mercy. It's from the Grinch. They have a whole Who Village on the west side of the park, complete with a green Grinch – after he found the Christmas spirit, of course."

We walked closer and listened for a while.

"They do this every hour, until Santa gets here, Mercy."

"We've got to get them in the parade, Ruby. It's too late to build a float for them, but maybe they can walk and sing."

"No worries, Mercy. Your assistant producer will get the lumberyard to loan us a flatbed. We just need a small tree and some white sheets or something to look like snow. I know the teacher who organized this, so consider it done!"

"That would be terrific! We'll put them next to last, right before Santa Claus. You're the best, Ruby!"

"No, Deloris is."

"What? But you weren't there when..."

"Oh, that's right. Let's go see Babs. I could use a bite."

Everything was fine at the Old School booth, so we had a nibble and decided to see how the hay wagon was coming.

"Hi, guys," I said to Jake and Junior, who were both kneeling next to the old wooden wagon, which they had standing on its side now. "I brought you a little snack."

"And I've got two fresh-squeezed lemonades for you from the Moonbucks booth," Ruby added, setting them down on top of an old 55-gallon drum.

"Looks like you're making some progress, boys."

"Well," Jake said, getting to his feet and brushing off his overalls, "we've pretty much completed the demolition portion."

"Yup," Junior agreed, his mouth already full. "We cut all the rusty parts off with the acetylene torch. So, now we just gotta put on the sleigh runners. Mm. These are good."

"I've been checking, Junior, because I was hoping for a white Christmas too. But it doesn't look like any snow is coming our way. Wheels might be a better idea."

"Well," he said, halfway through his lemonade now, "there was just a big storm in the Gulf the other day, so I figure all that moisture should come up this way and run right into that cold front coming in from Minnesota. We could get a foot of snow if everything comes together just right."

I looked at Ruby. "I guess Junior is a meteorologist now."

"Sounds like it could work," Ruby said with a shrug.

"But, you guys, I think St. Louis is supposed to get the snow, and maybe Chicago."

"Don't worry," Junior told us, taking the last bite of his snack. "I talked to Ed Bear. He's a Chickasaw chief. He's going to take care of it. They're having a powwow tonight in front of the Christmas tree. His rain dance ended the draught two summers ago, so it should work for snow too."

"Well, tell him to take it easy. We don't want to have to cancel the parade on account of too much snow," I said with my tongue in my cheek.

"Oh! Yeah, good idea. I'll tell him." Junior walked over to a few loose bales of hay by the wall, yawning as he went. "I'm going to take a little nap and then get into my new Santa suit."

"The kids are going to love it," I said excitedly.

"Yeah, the kids loved Snata in the red pajamas. Hopefully the parents won't be mad at me tonight." He sat down and fluffed up some of the hay for a pillow.

"Trust me, Junior. Nobody will be mad at you tonight – and the kids are going to be more excited than you've ever seen them."

He nodded and went to sleep.

Junior was on fire tonight in his new Santa suit. He really did seem to be the genuine jolly old soul, and he was attracting a lot of attention. At one point, when the band was playing, he even got up on the stage and did some terrific break dancing, spinning on his back and head. He even did the splits!

"This might be my favorite night ever at the

festival, Ruby," I told her as we heard the tom-toms start beating for the powwow. "Whoville was terrific, Junior is amazing, and now they're starting the powwow. We should get Ed Bear in the parade too. I can't think of anything that could make this night better!"

"Hi, girls. Got room for one more in your group?"

Well, maybe Brody could make the night even better. He seemed to appear out of nowhere, wearing his Sheriff's uniform.

"I think we can squeeze you in, Brody. Looks like you're on duty. How's the case coming?"

We all sat on a bench not too far from the Chickasaw bonfire and dancing.

"Theoretically, I just got off, but you know how it is when there's an active case. We really need to get this guy before he kills someone else, but the evidence is not really adding up to anything yet."

"Did you try to find out who bought those canes and the blades he used to modify them?"

"Well, that's just it, Mercy. He stole the canes from people here at the festival. They are a well-made novelty item that someone is selling in the Christmas Village. We know there are at least two other people who said they bought one and it was stolen, but nobody saw the thief."

"But the festival just started yesterday. He had to put those blades on the canes first, and that must have taken some work."

"True. The vendor said he had a boxful stolen a week or so ago too, at a flea market a half hour south of here."

"How many are in a box?" Ruby asked him.

"Six. Just not sure what ties Ed Greely and the professor at the college together, though."

"Well," I said, "Ed was in TV news, and the professor taught media, didn't she?"

"Oh, yeah, mass communications. Is that media?"

"So, look for one of her students who went to work at Channel 7."

"And who has some woodworking skills and knows how to engrave," Brody said with a pensive nod. "The professor's name, Andrea Hern, was engraved on the blade that killed her, just like Ed Greely. I think you've given me some direction now, Mercy. Thanks."

Brody's phone rang, and he listened for a long moment. Then he hung up and jumped to his feet. He shook his head and exhaled.

"Another body, Mercy. Same MO. This guy is on a killing spree."

"Oh, no. Where? Who?"

He didn't answer right away. Then he looked at me.

"The reporter, Maria Brown-Calderon. At the Channel 7 Christmas party."

Chapter Six

The next day Brody called me just as the noon bells started ringing at St. Catherine's.

"Hi, Brody! Got time for lunch? The empanadas are made, Babs is off and running to the festival, my produce order is emailed in, and I'm ready for a nice soup and salad. Meet me at Rocco's?"

"Sorry, sweetheart. I just wanted to tell you that there's been another incident."

"Oh, no. Another murder already this morning, Brody?"

"Not exactly. The victim got away."

"Ooh! Well that's a relief. Please tell me it wasn't in Paint Creek."

He paused for a while. "Well...okay, then...it was in Whoville."

"Whoville! You mean the little village at the festival? Are the children okay?"

"Everybody's fine, Mercy. They were just starting to set things up around 10:00 a.m. when the maniac attacked."

"Who? Who did he attack?"

"He went after the Grinch, just after he had gotten into his costume. Fortunately, they had used some kind of papier-mâché form and lots of padding to shape and reinforce costume. The blade got stuck halfway through and gave the guy time to react. Never broke the kid's skin. It just said *The Grinch* on the blade."

"Well, that was lucky."

"The kid in the costume was a football player from the high school, and he took a couple of swings and kicks at the assailant. Without the shielding from the costume, he said the surprise attack probably would have killed him."

"Wow. Can he identify him?"

"The attacker flipped the lights off in the dressing room, and there were no windows. So, all he can say is that it was a male, average height, maybe in his 20s or 30s. He was wearing a hoodie."

“Well, let me know when you can take a short break. And Brody...”

“Yes?”

“Catch this guy.”

The next few days were very tense for the little town of Paint Creek, and I’m sure for the whole area. A serial killer was on the loose, and it was really putting a damper on the Christmas mood.

The close-call in Whoville may have been what caused the killer to take a break for the past three days, but everyone was still on high-alert. Tomorrow was Christmas Eve, and I prayed we could make it through the holiday without any more tragedies. And I had a lot of practical matters to worry about.

The sleigh was still a work in progress with the big parade just a day away, and still no sign of an impending blizzard. I dropped into the big barn in mid-afternoon to see how the guys were doing and offer some moral support.

“Brody!” I said happily. “What are you doing here?”

“Actually, I’m not sure, Mercy. I guess I’m just everywhere you want me to be.”

The old wagon didn't look much different than it did a few days ago, except for the addition of a couple of steel runners so it could glide through the, well, pavement. I was thinking that Santa might have to walk through the parade.

"Are you going to get this thing ready on time, guys? The parade is tomorrow. It's not even painted yet."

"It'll be done," Junior said confidently, but his dad just shook his head and shrugged.

"Hey, Mercy, did you bring any food today?" Junior asked.

"Sorry, actually, no. But I can run to the booth in a while."

"That's okay. I need something different for a change. I really wish I had a nice ham sandwich."

I looked at his Santa suit lying in the corner. "Try your front pocket," I said, pointing to the suit.

"Huh?"

I brought the suit jacket to him and held it open for him to slip into. His hair and beard grew white and long, and I patted his front pocket, where he had gotten my Kit Kat bar from.

"Here," I said.

He reached in and pulled out the ham sandwich of his dreams.

Brody looked confused but seemed afraid to ask about the white hair. "You keep a ham sandwich in your pocket, Junior?"

"Not exactly," he said, sliding it back in the pocket, but still holding onto it.

"What are you doing?" Jake asked him.

"Adding mustard and tomatoes."

He took the completed sandwich out and tore it neatly into two pieces. "Here, Pops."

"We'll let you two eat," I said, grabbing Brody's arm and heading out the door. "Bye!"

"Did anything in there seem odd to you, Mercy?"

"Nothing is odd when the Carter men are involved," I said, deflecting the question as best I could. "Let's find a bench, and you can tell me where you're at with the case."

We must have talked for half an hour. He felt like he was making headway, but he couldn't find the evidence he needed to make an arrest.

"I did find a guy who was interning at the station for Greely," Brody told me, "and he did have

Hern for a semester. She gave him a grade of D for the class."

"That sounds like a good lead."

"I thought so too, but we raided his little apartment in town and found nothing. No candy canes or blades, no receipts, no woodworking or engraving tools."

"Does he have an alibi?"

"He was working the camera here for Ed the night of the first murder, and he was at the Channel 7 Christmas Party, so yes and no."

"Hmm. Did you check his laptop or Facebook page?"

He nodded. "Nothing."

"How about his phone? And is he a local kid? Maybe he still has a room at his parents' place."

He looked at me. "Are you sure you're a nurse and not a detective, Mercy Howard?"

"Just your humble assistant, Dr. Watson, at your service, Sheriff."

"Well, I'm going to get a warrant for his phone and for his parents' house, if they live in the area. Are you planning on staying here all day, or do you want to meet me at Rocco's at 7:00 or

8:00?"

"Rocco's at 8:00! I've got some final inspections to do for the parade." I answered enthusiastically. "We can share a family platter of spaghetti and meatballs."

"Now you're talking! See you at 8:00!"

Ruby had been a huge help in making the final preparations for the Parade of Lights tomorrow. I checked the last five floats, which were in a big hangar across from the park. I tested their lights and made sure they would fit under the footbridge over 4th street. When I checked off the last detail, I called Ruby to see how she was coming along with her list.

"All done!" she said. "Isn't it exciting? Just one day left till Christmas, and the parade is all set to go!"

"It is exciting! I thought this parade was going to drag down my mood, but it's really made Christmas better than ever. Ruby, put on something nice. I'm going to go home and change, and I'll pick you up in about an hour. Since we got everything finished up early, I'm taking you to the Oasis in Calhoun for Happy Hour, and then you're going to join Brody and me for spaghetti and meatballs at Rocco's!"

Silence.

"Spaghetti? You mean like carbohydrates all covered with, um, red meat?"

Oh, boy. "You can have the lentil soup and a Caesar's salad with no dressing, if you prefer."

"Oh, that sounds good!"

It does? Maybe if you're a rabbit.

"Great!"

Before I knew it, Ruby and I were making our grand entrance at the Oasis. She was in a ruby red over-the knee vintage Valentino dress with cherry-bomb red lipstick and red Jimmy Choo heels. I opted for the LBD that I wore to the County's Christmas party at the Radisson a couple weeks ago.

"You are classic Audrey Hepburn in that little black dress, girl," Ruby whispered to me as we strutted past the stares and leers of half the businessmen in Calhoun.

"Except she was a petite brunette, and I'm...not. But I think we got their attention," I told her. "Let's sit at the bar and flirt with the bartender."

"Mercy! No! Well...okay! It might be fun."

We were both engaged and totally loyal to our men, but we were looking good, and it felt good to be noticed.

The bartender walked right up to us the moment we sat and locked eyes with Ruby.

"Good evening, Miss. What can I get for you and your mother?"

I slammed both hands down on the bar without even thinking. "Let's move to the table in the corner, Ruby. We'll order from the waitress."

We moved, and Ruby was all giggles.

"Mother!" I said indignantly. "Do I look like your mother, Ruby?"

She shook her head but continued to laugh.

"I'm 33 years old..."

"You're 34 now, Mercy."

"And you're 26."

"I'm 27."

"How in the world could I be your mother? Am I wrinkled? Are my fashions that out of date?"

"Relax, Mercy! I think you just made him say that because you felt guilty about wanting to flirt."

“What? Made him say that? That’s crazy talk. And how on earth would he know what I was thinking or feeling, Ruby?”

“We all do! One Strawberry-Appletini, please.” She said to the waitress.

“And I’ll have an Old-Fashioned. Wait!” That sounded like a drink for old people. “Make it two of those sickeningly sweet strawberry thingies that she just ordered.”

We talked for an hour, nursing one drink. Ruby told me that her fiancé, a famous rodeo cowboy, would be coming in for New Year’s. She was really excited about that, of course.

“What did you get Brody for Christmas, Mercy?”

“I never know what to get that man. I got him tickets for a show at the Civic Center Auditorium.”

“Tickets? You got your man tickets?”

“Yup – for a monster truck show and a barbecue festival in the parking lot there, first week of April.”

“Well, I guess that’s not so bad. I got Justin a pair of snakeskin cowboy boots. His old leather ones are kind of worn out.”

“Nice. And I also got Brody a spendy little putter he’s had his eye on for a while.”

“Lead with the putter, Merse. Guys like real...*things.*”

“He’s going to like the monster truck show too, Ruby. It’s kind of like a rodeo, but with trucks.”

We got to Rocco’s a little early and ordered an appetizer.

“A nice bruschetta sounds good,” Ruby said, perusing the menu.

“It does – but isn’t that bread? You know, carbohydrates?”

“Yeah, but it’s crunchy and covered with fresh herbs and veggies.”

“Ooh! The Cali-terranean sounds good. It’s got the roma tomatoes and basil and parmesan with kalamata olives and feta, like the Mediterranean, plus a little avocado. And, of course, balsamic.”

“Yum! Sold!”

It was delicious, and it wasn’t easy to save one for Brody, who walked in at 8:00 sharp.

He was whistling silently and had a bounce in his step I hadn’t seen in a while. And he wasn’t in uniform!

"Hey, hey! Both of my favorite ladies are here!" He gave Ruby a little smooch on the forehead and I got the usual peck on the cheek. "Is that bread thingy for me?"

He took a bite without waiting for a response.

"Mmm. Tastes like pretentious Millenialism and West Coast snobbery all rolled into one." He tossed the rest in his mouth and practically swallowed it whole.

"So, you seem to be in a particularly good mood tonight, Brody," I said. "Did you have a good day, or are you just happy to see us?"

"Well, I'm always happy to see you, of course, but..." He smiled deviously and raised his eyebrows twice.

"Was there a break in the case?" Ruby asked with a tone of excitement.

"You might say that. Acting on a tip from a brilliant diner owner, we searched his parents' house about 30 minutes from here. Actually, very close to that flea market the cane guy was at last week."

"Really! What did you find?"

"Well, his dad is a woodworker and had a garage full of table saws, routers, and hand tools of every kind. But the motherlode was in the basement in a trombone case under the kid's bed."

"A trombone case, huh? Let me guess – three more candy cane walking canes..."

"And three blades identical to the ones used in the murders with the names of more intended victims already engraved on them. Plus, an electric engraving tool, with his fingerprints all over it. Ladies, the Case of the Candy Cane Killer has been solved, and the perp is in the hoosegow awaiting arraignment. Our serial killer is no longer a threat."

"That is wonderful news!" Ruby squealed. "I feel so much better already!"

"We all do, Brody," I said with a sincere smile as I stroked the back of his head. "Great work. I'm so proud of you."

"I couldn't have done it without you!"

We heard a cheer go up from the bar area, and I leaned over to see that they were just getting the news of the arrest from the TV.

Rocco came to the table himself to bring a small bottle of champagne for the Sheriff.

This was going to be a really great Christmas after all.

"Mercy," Brody said, drawing my attention to the window.

I looked outside.

“Oh, my gosh! Are those snowflakes?”

“Well, there are definitely white things falling from the sky!”

“Oh, I hope it keeps up overnight.”

“There aren’t a lot of flakes yet,” Ruby said, “but I’ve got a feeling that we’re going to have a White Christmas – or at least a White Christmas Eve!”

Chapter Seven

The snow did keep up overnight, and by morning there was a beautiful two-inch blanket on the ground and trees. By noon, there were almost four inches. By the time the snow stopped falling at 5:00 p.m. we had six inches on the ground and a perfect temperature of 25 degrees.

It was a miracle.

With the Candy Cane Killer in custody, the sidewalks along the parade route were already filling up with spectators from every town within an hour of Paint Creek.

"One hour till the parade!" I hollered out to everyone as Ruby and I got all the participants lined up in the proper order. The bands and floats and cars filled up the entire street around the circle, and the groups that were walking were standing inside the park next to the exhibit they followed.

Ed Bear's group of rain dancers were all attired in their ceremonial garb and headdresses, and two Chickasaw boys were holding a big base drum horizontally for the drummer to beat. Several beautifully clad young girls held the banner in front of the group.

Not far away, where the last group in the circle met the first, the Whoville choir was warming up on a flat bed float that looked like it had been worked on for weeks.

"Great job on the Whoville float, Ruby."

She just smiled, and I could tell she was very proud of it.

A boy in uniform with a tuba under his arm was running toward the front of the park.

"Slow down, Roger! The high school marching band is right here. Don't run; you've got plenty of time."

Lucille Gildemeister walked through the array of floats and marching groups and decorated automobiles.

"Looks like everything is perfect and on schedule, Mercy. Great job! But I don't see Santa," she said craning her neck in every direction.

"Oh, we don't want to bring him out until it's time for him to join the parade at the very end. Don't want to spoil the climax," I said. "Junior is all set and waiting for his cue in the barn."

"Excellent." She gave me a smile and a nod and continued her walk through the floats.

"That was kind of a whopper, wasn't it, Mercy?" Ruby whispered to me.

"Maybe they're done now. Let's go check in on Jake and Junior."

There were loud crashes and bangs coming from inside the barn, and we could see flashing lights coming out from every crack around the door. They had put a sign on the door, *Keep Out! Men at Work.*

"Junior!" I hollered out, banging on the door. "Let me in!"

I heard everything stop for a moment, and he came closer to the door. "Sorry, Mercy. We don't have a welder's mask for you. You'll be blinded forever if you come in here now. But don't worry. We'll be done in an hour or so."

His calm voice did sound reassuring, but my stomach was tied up in knots.

"Junior, the parade begins in less than an hour now! You have to just stop working now and take the sleigh out the way it is. We need to get you lined up."

"We're last," he hollered. "We'll be fine. We're almost finished."

"I need Brody," I told Ruby.

"I'm here," he said, walking up, in uniform. "Let the guys work for a while, Mercy. It won't help anybody for you to fret and worry and give yourself an ulcer over this."

"But..."

"And if they are still in there when the band starts the parade, I'll shoot my way in and pull them out of there."

I couldn't hold back a reluctant laugh.

"I guess you're right. Let's make sure everything else is ready."

"It's just about dark now," Ruby said. "Let's get everyone lighted up."

"That's a good idea."

"Yes, and it's in the instructions to get all the lights on a half-hour before the parade."

"Oh, so let's do that then."

We walked toward the band at the front of the circle.

"You're looking very dapper tonight," I said to Brody.

"Well, this is my dress uniform, since you insisted that you add me as the Grand Marshall."

"Well, the whole town insisted on it after you arrested the serial killer and saved Christmas. You'll be right in front of the band, in my classic Mercedes. It's the only convertible left within 50 miles of here. Your deputy, Stan, is going to drive."

"You should be riding with me, since, you know, you're my queen *and* you figured out how to solve the case."

"I'll stay in the shadows, thanks. And, besides, I have a parade to run. But I'll need your gun."

"Excuse me?"

"Well, you're at the front of the parade, so you won't be able to shoot your way into the barn when the band starts playing."

"Funny. I left my squirt gun on the dresser at home. But, if I know my girl, you'll have no trouble getting in there if you really have to."

"I suppose so."

Deputy Stan Doggerty jogged up to us. “Time to go, Sheriff!”

“Oh, my gosh!” I looked at my watch, and it was just five minutes before the parade would begin. “It seems like this past hour has gone in just a few minutes! Stan, you’re first, so you set the pace. Four miles per hour. Brody, you keep an eye on the marching band behind you so you can tell him if he needs to speed up or slow down. Square corners at the intersections. I hope you know the route.”

“I better,” Stan said. “I set up all the road blocks for the event this afternoon. At 15 minutes per mile, we should be back here in about 45 minutes. How’s your car in the snow? You wouldn’t let them plow the streets.”

“Not good,” I told him, “but it’s a light fluffy snow. I didn’t have any problem getting here. Go, now! Get in the car!”

I took one long, deep breath and looked around the perimeter of the circle at all the beautiful blinking, flashing, twinkling, and dazzling lights. It was a wondrous sight to behold.

The head majorette looked over at Ruby and me as the band members all held out an arm to get the right distance to the person in front of them.

“It’s time,” Ruby said.

"Give her the thumbs up, then. Let's do this!"

"You should be the one to start the parade, Mercy."

One more deep breath, and I gave the girl three fingers, two fingers, one finger...then I pointed at her.

She pointed her baton straight up and blew her whistle.

Tweeeeeeeeeet! Tweet! Tweet Tweet!

The drums began to beat; then the trumpets sounded, and batons began to twirl. The majorettes all did a high kick, and then the band began to march in perfect synchronization, with Brody leading the way as Grand Marshall.

There was a huge cheer from the crowd on Main Street as the half-mile long parade began to leave the park.

"You can exhale now, Mercy," Ruby said, holding up her hand for a high-five. "You did it!"

It felt so good. "We did it."

Then I got a panicked look on my face.

"Mercy, you go check on Santa. I'll get everybody marching on time."

I started to reply, but I she stopped me.

"I know, I know. I'm the best."

Ruby cranked out float after float, and I knew I had only minutes to get Junior out of the barn. A half-mile long parade moving at 4 miles an hour only gave me seven-and-a-half minutes, and two of those were already gone. I ran like the wind.

"Junior! Junior! I need you now! Right now!" I hollered loudly as I banged on the door.

"One second, Mercy."

"No! Please! We're out of time!"

Suddenly I heard bells jingling and some really good ho-ho-hos.

"Get away from the door, now, Mercy Howard! I don't want to run over my favorite little girl!"

I backed away just as the door flew open, and eight reindeer with jingle-bell collars came whooshing out of the barn. They were pulling the most spectacular sleigh I had ever seen!

It was bright red with gold runners and trim, with a huge sack of gifts stashed in the back. Junior pulled on the reins to stop the animals. He looked like the perfect Santa, and Jake was the perfect elf on the seat next to him.

I gasped and could hardly speak. "Junior, where did you get reindeer?"

"They're horses, Mercy. They just look like reindeer."

"But..."

"We'll talk later, Mercy Howard. Santa has to go! Merrrrry Christmas!"

He gently whipped the reindeer, and they trotted off, getting to the edge of the circle just as the Whoville choir started to make its way down Main Street.

Then it dawned on me: I was done. Everyone in the parade was on the route now. I could stop worrying.

I walked slowly back to Ruby at the front of the circle, and she was really pleased. She gave me a hug.

"Everything went off without a hitch, Mercy, and the crowd is loving it. You should have seen the kids when Santa came by in that beautiful sleigh."

A few flakes of snow started gently falling again.

"I guess Ed Bear's snow dance worked, Ruby. We're going to have a White Christmas!"

"Everything worked, Mercy! Now all we have to do is wait for everyone to get back."

"I guess so. We'd better make sure that Babs is ready for the big rush after the parade."

"Are you kidding me? Babs is always ready, and Deloris is going to help her. Red is going to pass out the candy tonight. Under the circumstances, they will be giving the kiddies red and green wrapped chocolate kisses instead of candy canes tonight."

I nodded. "Good idea, I suppose. But I'm always going to love my candy canes."

"Me too."

The time passed quickly, and we could hear the high school band making its way back to the circle, playing *Carol of the Bells*. The crowd at the park started gathering around the perimeter to watch them make their final round.

I waved to Brody as he entered the loop. He looked like he had been enjoying the experience.

"Ruby, I'm going to find a place to sit down. I'm feeling a little funny."

"Are you sick?" She asked, escorting me to the nearest bench.

"No, nothing like that. I think it's like I'm

losing all my energy all of a sudden."

"You poor girl. You're probably just starving. Did you eat today?"

"I don't know. I don't remember."

"Hi, ladies!" Brody found us at our bench. "Are you okay, Mercy?"

"I'm fine now, Brody. Just a little post-parade syndrome. How was it?"

"I've never seen the streets of Paint Creek lined with so many people! It was amazing. Lucille looked very pleased in the judges' booth halfway through, too. Pretty sure you're going to get a great review and probably a call-back for next year."

"Looks like Santa's sleigh held up through the three-mile route," Ruby said.

Junior entered the loop, standing and waving from his sleigh. "Ho ho ho! Merry Christmas. Merrrrry Christmas!"

"Brody, are those reindeer or horses?"

He laughed and then saw my serious expression. "They're horses, Mercy. Reindeer are smaller and have antlers."

I was definitely seeing reindeer.

"Yeah, I know. I'm just so exhausted all of a sudden that I think I was hallucinating for a minute."

"Come on," he said. "Let's head to the barn and meet Junior when he gets there. He deserves a nice warm reception."

"He does."

I could feel my head spin a little when I stood up, but I didn't want to alarm anybody. I was sure it was nothing. We arrived at the barn just as Junior was pulling up in the sleigh.

"Great job, Junior!" Ruby said.

"Yes, you were terrific," Brody added.

"Junior, you...the sleigh...everything was just wonderful. Thank you so much."

"Ho ho. No need for thanks. That's Santa's job! Now, if you will excuse me, it's Christmas Eve! Santa's got to make his rounds around the entire world. The children are waiting! Merry Christmas to all!" Then he shook the reins. "On Dasher, on Dancer, on Comet and Cupid – and the rest of you too!"

I didn't really know where he was going, but the sleigh took off, gliding through the snow, bells jingling and snow falling. Then everything got really strange.

When the sleigh reached the edge of the circle, I could swear I saw it leave the ground and start flying through the sky.

Okay, now I know I'm hallucinating.

Brody was talking to Ruby, paying no attention to the sleigh, but I could still see the sleigh rising higher and higher into the night sky.

I needed my anchor. "Brody," I said shaking his arm, but he paid no attention. "Brody, look! Tell me if I'm crazy. Brody! Brody! Brody!"

Chapter Eight

"Mercy...Mercy...Mercy!"

I could feel someone shaking my shoulder, and I could hear Brody's voice. But it seemed like he was a million miles away. I think I was kicking my feet, but I just didn't know. I just kept calling his name.

"Mercy...shhh...shhh, now Mercy...Mercy...wake up!"

I bolted forward into an upright sitting position. I opened my eyes, but it took a minute for me to focus. Where was I?

My jaw was practically on my chest, and I looked to see all my friends. "Brody. Ruby."

Everyone was there. Deloris and Babs, Jake

and Junior, Red and Smoke. And other people in white uniforms were there too. There was an IV bag dripping into one of my arms and monitors hooked up to various parts of my body.

"I'm...in...the hospital? Why? I'm perfectly fine."

"Yes," Brody reassured me. "You're perfectly fine, Mercy. It's just a precautionary measure. You were totally exhausted and extremely dehydrated. I'm sorry I wasn't paying enough attention to notice how worn out you were in time, Mercy," his voice cracked and he gave me a tight smile, trying to hide a tear of guilty concern.

"Don't be silly. I'm a grown woman, and a nurse. I don't expect anyone else to look out for my wellbeing. But when? How long?"

"You collapsed in my arms right after we found Ed Greely."

"Yes, I know, but that was just for a minute, and almost a week ago."

"No!" I said when I saw a young man behind all my friends holding a camera above the people to get a shot of me.

"The station just wants one shot of the woman who passed out next to our, um, unfortunate anchorman," I heard him whisper to Ruby.

"It was three hours ago, Mercy; not a week," Brody said, squeezing my hand. "Sylvia and Stan would be here, but they're working on Ed's murder," he said, regarding Medical Examiner Sylvia Chambers and Deputy Stan Doggerty. "They send their regards."

"Don't be silly, Brody. You already solved the case and arrested the Candy Cane Killer."

"The Candy Cane Killer?"

"Yes. It was Ed Greely's cameraman, that intern kid from the college. You found the name of all six of his planned victims on his phone and all the physical evidence you needed at his parent's house."

"Excuse me," I heard someone say trying to make their way to the door. "Excuse me."

"That guy," I said pointing to the young man with the camera.

He got to the door and was just about to start running down the hall, but Junior grabbed the back of his shirt. Deloris reached into my purse on the chair in the corner and pulled out my little .38 Baretta.

"He's not going anywhere, Sheriff," Deloris said.

Brody made his way to the killer and

handcuffed him. Then he pushed him into the corner. Jake and Junior stood in front of him, arms folded.

"Mercy, I want to stay here with you, but I've got to bring this prisoner in – and I'm going to need a lot more information from you, like how you knew who the killer was."

"That's fine, Brody. And I'm feeling much, much better now. Really."

"I can see in your face and eyes that you're almost your old self," he said. But I'll be back as soon as I can."

"How about you just take care of business and be back here first thing in the morning to take me home. And make sure you get here before they force that hospital breakfast on me!"

He smiled. "Now I know you're feeling better."

As soon as Brody left, a man appeared at the door with a large red box.

"Is there a Jake Carter, Junior here?" He asked.

The man looked familiar, but I couldn't place him.

"That's me," Junior said, stepping toward the

man.

"Sir, we've been getting calls from all the people in Paint Creek and Calhoun telling us about the wonderful Santa Claus who had no Santa Claus suit. The people at the festival directed us here. On behalf of Magical Novelties, Inc. I would like to present you with our deluxe Kris Kringle suit."

"Gee, thanks!" Junior said, taking the large box.

"Now, if you will just sign here, indicating that you received the item," he said putting on his glasses.

Those spectacles... "Ferdy?

"Miss? I'm Alex Ferdinand. I haven't been Ferdy since high school wrestling. Have we met."

"No...no, sorry."

He took the receipt from Junior, bowed his head slightly to each of us, and was gone.

"I'm sure you're going to love that suit, Junior. It will help you really get into character."

"He opened the box and looked at it. It's really a nice suit, Mercy. Not sure why they just gave it to me."

"That's what happens when you're the best

Santa Claus in the business. How's that sleigh coming?"

"Geez, I don't know, Mercy. All the snow is gone already. Maybe we'll just do hay rides."

"No way. I heard there was a storm in the Gulf, so there might be a lot of moisture coming up this way. Why don't you ask Ed Bear to do a rain dance, except for snow?"

His face lit up. "That's a great idea! That'll work for sure."

"Great, because I'm going to need Santa's sleigh in my parade."

"Your parade?"

A woman walked into the room, and I recognized her as Lucille Gildemeister.

"I heard they brought you here, and I just had to come to wish you the best."

"Oh, hi, Lucille. I'm doing fine now. And, of course, it's your parade. But, you know if Marcy calls you and decides to go skiing at Aspen this week, I'm your girl!"

Her phone rang. Her face went blank and she looked at me before she hung up.

"Marcy's going to Aspen. So, I can count on

you then?"

"Done deal," I said, "as long as Ruby will be my assistant producer."

"I'd love to!" Ruby said, genuinely.

A nurse walked into the room. I couldn't see her behind all the people, but I could hear her.

"Okay, everyone, time to go. Miss Howard needs her rest, and then you can have her back in the morning!"

Everyone said their goodbyes, and I yawned.

"One good night's sleep, and I should be 100 percent, I said to the nurse as she changed the IV bag."

"And one more bag of fluid," she said with a smile.

Oh, my. "Cupcake?"

She gave me an odd look. "My dad used to call me that." She let out a little giggle. "Actually, he still does. He even made 35 cupcakes for me last month on my 35th birthday."

I just nodded. *Maybe I'm still hallucinating*.

"But, you're a girl."

"That I am!" She said, giving me an odd look.

Then she pretended to grab something out of the palm of her hand with the fingertips of her other hand, sprinkling the invisible stuff on me.

"What's that?" I asked.

She gently tucked her flaxen hair behind a rather pointy ear. "Pixie dust. For good luck." She winked and pulled my covers up just a little before she left the room.

I insisted that the whole gang come over to my house after dinner on Christmas Day. Six inches of snow on Christmas Eve, and another inch overnight made it one of the best Christmases I could remember.

Of course, Smoke, Ruby, and Brody came to my house for dinner too. Smoke loved to make holiday dinners, and I wasn't going to complain! His turkey with all the trimmings was wonderful.

And, naturally, Ruby was busy now making some goodies for dessert with the whole group.

Deloris and Babs made dinner at Deloris's house for the rest of the gang. The bell rang, and everybody arrived together.

"I hope you're all not tired of wassail yet,"

Deloris said, bringing in a five-quart crockpot filled with the liquid gold.

"Never!" I said, taking the pot right to the serving table we had set up in the living room. "Your wassail is perfect all the time, especially on Christmas Day."

Ruby already had a platter of Christmas cookies on the table, and another of beautifully decorated gingerbread men. She came in from the kitchen now with yet another treat.

"Here' you go, folks," She said with a bright smile as she set another platter down. "Snickerdoodle candy cane cookies with red and white peppermint icing!"

"More candy canes? Really, Ruby?" I asked, though they did make my mouth water.

"Well you were the only one who got to have a Candy Cane Killer and a big candy cane Danish, Mercy. It's only fair."

"Speaking of which," Brody said, "we've barely had a minute to talk since you cracked that case, what with the festival and the parade and all."

"Yeah," I said. "Solving that murder didn't leave you with much of a case load."

"Hey, now. My team provided security for festivals all over the county."

“Just teasing, Sheriff,” I said with a smile. “It was just a lucky fluke.”

“Was it though?” He had a serious look on his face. “I mean, you nailed just about every detail, Mercy. The names on the list, the canes that were stolen from the flea market – I was chasing the canes that were stolen at the festival here, but those turned out to just be random thefts. And then, of course, searching his parents’ house instead of his apartment.”

“Well, the best part is that Professor Hern and Maria Brown-Calderone are still alive,” I said. “That makes it worthwhile to feel like I’m insane.”

“Let’s just chalk it all up to a Christmas miracle,” Ruby said, raising her glass of wassail.

“I’ll drink to that,” Junior said, raising a big mug.

“Me too,” echoed Jake and the others.

Somehow, this had turned out to be the best Christmas ever. I knew in this moment that I really was with family right now. These people were the world to me, and Paint Creek was my home forever. There was no doubt about that.

Of course, although I told them every detail of my dream, I didn’t tell them that I saw Ferdy and Cupcake at the hospital. That was just too crazy for me to share.

But I did save some of that invisible pixie dust she sprinkled on me and put it in my coin purse, because – you just never know.

*****

My grandmother and her church family put together a recipe book in 1950. My other grandmother was the President of the Ladies Homemaker Club in her hometown and they also put together a recipe book in about the same time period. Although the books are weathered with wear, I'm sure the recipes are still good today. Here is a recipe from my grandmother, Lorene Forgey. Enjoy!

Chocolate Fudge Cake

Ingredients:

2 cups sifted flour

3 teaspoons baking powder

1/2 teaspoon soda

1/4 teaspoon salt

1/2 cup butter

1 cup sugar

2 egg yolks, beaten

3 squares Baker's unsweetened chocolate

1 1/4 cups milk

1 teaspoon vanilla

2 egg whites, stiffly beaten

Sift flour once, measure again, then add baking powder, soda and salt. Sift the mixture 3 times. Cream the butter, then add the sugar gradually and cream together until light and fluffy. Add egg yolks one at a time and beat after each addition until smooth. Add vanilla and add in egg whites. Pour mixture into two greased 9-inch layer pans. Bake at 350 degrees for 30 minutes or until an inserted toothpick in the middle of the cake comes out clean. Allow the cakes to cool before icing.

Icing

Ingredients:

1 1/2 cups powdered sugar

1 teaspoon of butter

2 tablespoons cocoa

1/2 teaspoon vanilla

1/2 cup hot coffee

Mix the first four ingredients together. Then add coffee 1 tablespoon at a time to make the icing soft enough to spread over the cakes.

Thanks for Reading

I hope you enjoyed the book and it would mean so much to me if you could leave a review. Reviews help authors gain more exposure and keep us writing your favorite stories.

You can find all of my books by visiting my Author Page.

Sign up for Constance Barker's New Releases Newsletter where you can find out when my next book is coming out and for special discounted pricing.

I never share or sell your email.

Visit me on Facebook and give me feedback on the characters and their stories.

Catalog of Books

Triplet Witch Sisters Mystery Series

Two's Company, Three's a Coven

Resting Witch Face

Bewitched and Bewildered

Triple Toil and Trouble

The Witch Sisters of Stillwater

Hoodoo and Just Desserts

A Shade of Murder

That Ol' Black Magic

A Whole Lotta Witchin Goin On

The Beast Cometh

Secrets and Sorcery

The Lucky Dill Deli Mystery Series

A Yuletide Wallop

Haunted Homicide

The Leprechaun's Loot

The Sinister Case Series

Mirror, Mirror Murder Them All

A Wicked Enchantment

A Scorching Spell

The Grumpy Chicken Irish Pub Series

A Frosty Mug of Murder

Treachery on Tap

A Highball and a Low Blow

Cursed With a Twist

A Whiskey Sour Wipeout

Old School Diner Cozy Mysteries

Murder at Stake

Murder Well Done

A Side Order of Deception

Murder, Basted and Barbecued

Murder Ala Mode

The Curiosity Shop Cozy Mysteries

The Curious Case of the Cursed Spectacles

The Curious Case of the Cursed Dice

The Curious Case of the Cursed Dagger

The Curious Case of the Cursed Looking Glass

The Curious Case of the Cursed Crucible

Witchy Women of Coven Grove Series

The Witching on the Wall

A Witching Well of Magic

Witching the Night Away

Witching There's Another Way

Witching Your Life Away

Witching You Wouldn't Go

Witching for a Miracle

Teasen & Pleasen Hair Salon Series

A Hair Raising Blowout

Wash, Rinse, Die

Holiday Hooligans

Color Me Dead

False Nails & Tall Tales

Caesar's Creek Series

A Frozen Scoop of Murder

Death by Chocolate Sundae

Soft Serve Secrets

Ice Cream You Scream

Double Dip Dilemma

Melted Memories

Triple Dip Debacle

Whipped Wedding Woes

A Sprinkle of Tropical Trouble

A Drizzle of Deception

Sweet Home Mystery Series

Creamed at the Coffee Cabana

A Caffeinated Crunch

A Frothy Fiasco

Punked by the Pumpkin

Peppermint Pandemonium

Expresso Messo

A Cuppa Cruise Conundrum

The Brewing Bride

Whispering Pines Mystery Series

A Sinister Slice of Murder

Sanctum of Shadows

Curse of the Bloodstone Arrow

Fright Night at the Haunted Inn

The Chronicles of Agnes Astor Smith

The Peculiar Case of Agnes Astor Smith

The Peculiar Case of the Red Tide

The Peculiar Case of the Lost Colony

Made in the USA
Middletown, DE
16 December 2021